WAITING

FOR

HIGH TIDE

Nikki McClure

Abrams Books for Young Readers

New York

WAITING FOR HIGH TIDE.

I close my eyes and open them.

Close and open.

Still low tide.

I squint and wait.

There is a big stretch of mud between me and the water's edge. I want to swim, but I'd just get muddy. Or worse. I'd get stuck, and Grandma would have to rescue me.

It seems like I spend every day all hot summer long waiting for the water to creep back over the mud. I'm not alone. Crabs under rocks, clams and worms burrowed deep, barnacles closed tight—they wait for high tide too. It takes six hours for the water to rise from low tide to high tide. That's a long time!

I WANT TO SWIM NOW.

INSTEAD, I SIT AND WAIT.

But it's not going to be so bad today.

TODAY WE ARE GOING TO BUILD A RAFT.

We found a big log drifting loose after a storm and towed it to our beach. Last night we cut it up into three sections. I had to stuff my fingers in my ears when Papa started the chainsaw.

The three smaller logs were too heavy to move with our hands alone. While the tide was high, Papa rolled the logs into the water, using a peavey as a lever. The logs floated. We easily lined them up side by side. Then the tide went out, and now the logs sit on the beach, waiting to become a raft.

Mama and Papa, even Grandma, are here to help.

We are not the only ones ready to work this morning . . .

Crows scan the morning high-tide line for useful tidbits. I follow them. "The sea provides," Mama says. The beach always has what you need. Maybe today there is pirate treasure.

I FIND:

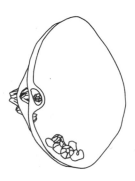

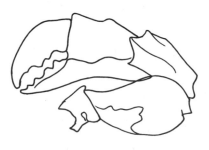

one fine long pole
four clamshells
miscellaneous crab parts
three dead jellyfish
green and brown seaweeds that pop
curved pieces of bark perfect to float . . .
and sink with a volley of rocks
a bedraggled heron wing feather
tiny bits of yellow plastic rope
a soggy shoe that does not match any in my collection
a true score—sunglasses with one lens gone and
the other covered with barnacles. Now I have Barnacle
Vision!

Oh, I have to get real glasses to help me see.

I DON'T WANT TO WEAR GLASSES.
I CAN SEE FINE ENOUGH.

I can see everything on this beach . . .

IS THE TIDE COMING IN?

I put on my barnacle glasses, and I still can't see from here. I step light and quick across the mud, taking a bridge of crushed clamshells out to piles of barnacle-covered rock exposed by the low tide. I call the biggest pile Big Crab Island. The smallest pile is Little Crab Island. Peeking under a rock, I spy a hundred crabs that rustle and scurry to hide. They prefer to wait for high tide in cool shadow safety.

Mama says that the rock piles are from ships that came here long ago. The sailors would dump the ballast of rocks and then fill the hull and decks with a heavy cargo of logs from the forests. The timber became the ship's ballast, steadying it for the sea journey home. The logs were used to build cities all along the Pacific coast. The crabs made their own city under the rocks left behind.

Look! With my Barnacle Vision, I can see that the tide isn't waiting for me. Soon Big Crab Island will really be an island—before it disappears under water. I dash back across the mud to higher ground.

MUDDY, BUT WITH BOTH SHOES STILL ON, I START WORK ON THE RAFT.

I haul the fine long pole I found over to Papa, and he cuts it into three fine short poles and lays them across the logs. Mama marks where they line up on the logs. Notches need to be chopped here. The poles will fit in the grooves. We will then tie the poles to the logs to hold the raft together.

With two hands on my hatchet's handle and my legs safely out of the way, I swing down and chop into the first log.

CHOP, CHIP, CHOP, CHIP, CHOP.

Three notches done and I need a rest. I pass the hatchet over to Mama, who gives a few chops and chips of her own.

I walk along a ribbon of barnacles that stripes the upper beach. They cover the big rocks here that the waves can't tumble.

When barnacles are young, they swim all over as part of the plankton that drift in the sea. They have only one eye. (Just like my barnacle glasses!) With it, they look for other barnacles. When they find them, they settle down and cement their heads to something solid and barnacly: rocks, docks, lost sunglasses. And there they stay.

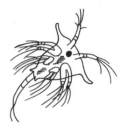

During low tide, the rocky beach gets hot and dry, but barnacles don't care. Their tough shells close tight, and they can breathe whether they're in or out of water. At high tide, barnacles feed. Tiny plates open, and feathered cirri (their legs!) swoop out to catch plankton (yes, little swimming barnacles, too). I could stare at them for hours and have the water cover me and still sit there watching them.

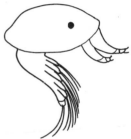

But the best part about barnacles is the noise they make. Miles and miles of tiny plates shifting about make a crackly, squizzling sound. Maybe they tell stories of all they saw with that one eye as they swam about in the world?

WHAT WILL I SEE?
WHAT STORIES WILL I TELL?

But first I need to work. I take my hatchet and chop. Chip, chop, chip.

THE TIDE CREEPS IN LITTLE BY LITTLE.

I chop and chip and listen to gulls squawking, "FOOD, FOOD, FOOD!"

I call out, "FOOD!" and then add "please," so my parents don't fly away. From Mama's handy picnic basket, I unpack peanut butter sandwiches, cold mint tea, and sweet watermelon.

We eat and talk and watch the gulls being followed relentlessly by their awkward gray young. They know that the incoming tide means food.

There are hidden treats under the mud. Hungry unseeing clams dig up from the mud to feed on plankton in the rising water. Gulls walk the waterline looking for them. Muddy beaks pry up the blackened shells.

Some gulls take a clam and fly in circles over the rocks . . . hover . . . and drop the shell. "Crack!" They flutter down to eat the soft clam inside before another gull swoops in.

Other gulls take a clam in beak and waddle up the shore. "Nothing to see here, folks." Then they hit the shell, once, twice—up to six times—on a rock to crack it open. When the clam inside is eaten, they waddle back to dig up more.

EVERYONE IS FEASTING:

clam, gull, human, and all the life in the mud
too small to see or fathom.

The tide creeps higher, and the barnacles start to feed. Under water, fish called sculpins zip about and crabs clean clam bits from gull–broken shells. A heron calmly lifts a leg high and cocks his head to one side, waiting for a sculpin to move. A sudden dart of sharp beak into the water; then he shakes his head and goes back to the silent stare and patient walk along the shore. How long will the sculpin lie still, camouflaged like a rock? This sculpin is willing to wait a bit more for the tide to come in and the water to deepen.

A boat goes by, and its wake rolls along the beach. The tide is rising. I put my sandwich down to finish chopping.

Mama sets poles across the notches I cut. Papa digs holes under the logs at each crossing point. Then he threads rope under and over the logs, under and over, under and over, and lashes the poles to the logs. If we nailed them together, the nails would snap as the logs rolled through white-capped winter storms and summers full of wild kids diving off all at the same time. Mama wedges a pry bar under the pole so Papa can pull even tighter. He then ties a knot. I chop the last notch.

OUR RAFT IS ALMOST DONE.

We need the tide to rise a bit higher before we can push the raft into the water. And we need a plank. I scout through piles of driftwood heaved up all winter and spy a board just the right size. A raft needs a plank for us to dive off of or be forced to walk by swimmers-turned-pirates. I drag the thick board over, and Papa lashes it on.

The raft is ready! The tide is not. So we nibble cookies and wait. A kingfisher rattles a warning to all fish in the sea and plunges into the water. Up he flies with a stickleback trapped in his beak, his wait over. The tide keeps rising. Big Crab Island is well under water. Crabs explore and feed freely. The mud flats are under water. Clams are safe from observant gulls. Sculpins swim, patrolling the mud for food.

MAYBE IT IS TIME?

I'VE WAITED SO LONG.

I WANT TO DIVE.

I WANT TO SWIM.

I put on my barnacle glasses and take a peek. The water is now only a foot away. I could wait for the water to lift the raft, but I've already waited all day! I grab a chunk of bark and start digging under the logs. "Help! Help!" I call. It will take more than me to get this raft moving. Mama, Papa, and even Grandma grab shovels and sticks and start digging to clear a way for the water under the raft. Water creeps under the first log, settling tiny stones and filling in the space. I keep digging. Tiny bits of clamshells and sand fly. Papa finds a stout pole in the driftwood stores. He tries to lever the raft down the beach, just a bit, to ride in the deepening water. He tries and tries. We all push, and maybe the raft shifts an inch, maybe not. It's just too heavy. It is crazy to think we can move this raft, but with each push we imagine that this is the push that will make the raft slip into the rising water.

Crows circle. Seals chasing fish stop to watch with shiny eyes. An eagle laughs overhead.

A breath of rest, and then we all push as hard as we can . . . and the raft moves! Another push, and it gives way.

THE RAFT IS FLOATING!

I hop on board, and the raft sways. Papa grabs some paddles, and everyone climbs on board. Kicking, splashing, laughing, we paddle the raft out to where it will be moored, just next to Big Crab Island over the mud flats. Papa ties the raft to an anchored buoy with a chain. Where he got this, I don't know. He is magic. This day of waiting is over. The water quiets around us. Bubbles in our wake pop and fade.

And whoops! Here we all are, Mama, Papa, Grandma, and me.

ON THE RAFT.

WITH ONLY ONE WAY BACK TO SHORE.

I take the first cannonball off the raft, followed by giant splashes. We swim ashore with paddles, with pants and shirts and hats and crazy smiling faces.

WE WAITED FOR HIGH TIDE. HERE IT IS.

We turn back and swim out to the raft and then jump off again and again and again.

Papa holds onto his glasses when he jumps so he doesn't lose them. I don't have to worry about that yet. My barnacle glasses enjoy the plunge. I think I can hear the barnacles happily feeding. I let the glasses drift off my face and sink to the bottom. Tomorrow I won't be able to find them. They will be gone, but the raft will still be here. Ready for me when the tide is high. I'll be waiting.

TO FINN AND ALL SWIMMERS
OF THE SALISH SEA

AUTHOR'S NOTE

We really did build a raft one summer. It's named the Leaky Kon-Tiki, for Thor Heyerdahl's intrepid vessel, and it has survived a few winters and summers. Now barnacles and mussels and even plumose anemones coat the undersides and filter the water as we swim about. Otters, herons, and ducks like to rest on it, and even Grandma. Once we lay on it so long that the tide went out under us and we walked off, across the mud. The raft floats at the southern end of the Salish Sea, near Olympia, Washington. You can find it on a map and look up the tide to see when it's high.

http://tidesandcurrents.noaa.gov
http://www.dairiki.org/tides/monthly.php/oly

P.S.

Yes, it is *my* hatchet. Please ask me before you use it. I am very careful with it and expect you to be the same. The rules are: Two hands on the hatchet at all times, legs out of the way; and that you must always put it away carefully after using it. And never leave it outside! If you leave it outside, I will never let you use my hatchet again.

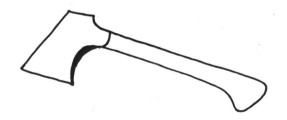

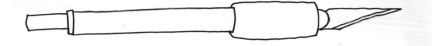

The illustrations in this book were made by cutting black paper
with an X-ACTO knife. I also used a fountain pen.

Library of Congress Cataloging-in-Publication Data

McClure, Nikki, author, illustrator.
Waiting for high tide / words and pictures by Nikki McClure.
pages cm
Summary: While waiting with family members for high tide to come in,
a youngster who is very knowledgeable about the seashore and what lives there
helps to build a raft.
ISBN 978-1-4197-1656-0
[1. Beaches—Fiction. 2. Marine animals—Fiction. 3. Tides—Fiction. 4. Family
life—Fiction.] I. Title.
PZ7.M4784141946Wai 2016
[E]—dc23
2015018203

Printed and bound in USA
10 9 8 7 6 5 4 3 2 1

Abrams Books for Young Readers are available at special discounts when purchased
in quantity for premiums and promotions as well as fundraising or educational
use. Special editions can also be created to specification. For details, contact
specialsales@abramsbooks.com or the address below.

THE ART OF BOOKS SINCE 1949

115 West 18th Street
New York, NY 10011
www.abramsbooks.com